D1243011

Turner, Morrie
            Nipper

NIPPER

NIPPER

by

MORRIE TURNER

Creator of WEE PALS

Foreword by
CHARLES SCHULZ

THE WESTMINSTER PRESS

Philadelphia

COPYRIGHT © MCMLXX MORRIE TURNER

ISBN 0-664-32464-9

LIBRARY OF CONGRESS CATALOG CARD NO. 77-97161

PUBLISHED BY THE WESTMINSTER PRESS ®
PHILADELPHIA, PENNSYLVANIA

PRINTED IN THE UNITED STATES OF AMERICA

To Patty and Morrie Junior

FOREWORD

There is a certain scene in this book that really sends
me. Little Nipper is given the opportunity to pitch,
but after a disastrous windup, he falls flat on his
face and is banished from the mound because he
does not have any rhythm. This is the sort of idea
that only Morrie Turner can come up with.

I think you will find a lot of incidents in this book
that will appeal to you in the same way this one did
to me.

Morrie's little kids have a way of speaking to all
of us, and I think you will find the climax clever,
touching, and a perfect solution to the problems that
are making our days so difficult.

CHARLES M. SCHULZ

CAN I HELP IT IF THERE'S A VOODOO CURSE ON ME?

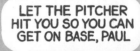